D1495728

Published by Scholastic Inc.
90 Old Sherman Turnpike, Danbury, Connecticut 06816.

For information regarding permission, write to:
Disney Licensed Publishing
114 Fifth Avenue, New York, New York 10011.

ISBN 0-7172-6818-7

Designed and produced by Bill SMITH STUDIO.

Printed in the U.S.A.
First printing, April 2004

No Strings Attached

A Story About
Generosity

by **Jacqueline A. Ball**
illustrated by
Teresa Lester *with* **S.I. International**

SCHOLASTIC INC.

New York Toronto London Auckland Sydney
Mexico City New Delhi Hong Kong Buenos Aires

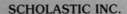

It was the Dwarfs' day off from the mine.
They were relaxing and doing chores.
Doc made a snack for Bashful and Sneezy.

Grumpy and Dopey carried in firewood.
Happy looked through his collections
and added string to the huge ball he had saved.
Meanwhile, Sleepy was napping upstairs.

$\mathcal{T}$here was a loud knock on the door.

"Who's there?" Grumpy called.

"I bring a message from Princess Snow White,"
a voice answered.

"The Princess!" the Dwarfs shouted.

Snow White had married the Prince and gone to live in his castle. The Dwarfs missed her very much, but she visited whenever she could.

They rushed to the door and pulled it open.

$\mathcal{A}$ messenger stood outside. He unrolled
a long scroll.

"Princess Snow White is planning a visit," he read

"Hooray!" cried all the Dwarfs at once.

"*W*hen will she be here?" asked Happy.

"The royal carriage will bring her tomorrow,"
replied the messenger.

"Tomorrow?" yawned Sleepy.

"Let's get to work!" said Grumpy.

As the Dwarfs prepared the cottage, they thought about Snow White's other visits.

Bashful and Grumpy thought about the baskets of food she brought.

Sleepy and Dopey remembered the bedtime stories she read to them.

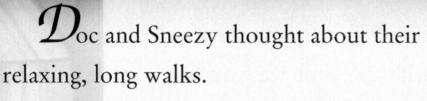

Doc and Sneezy thought about their relaxing, long walks.

Happy remembered the kind, useful gifts she brought them.

"Snow White is so generous," Happy said to himself. "It's time we gave her something, too. But what?"

$\mathcal{H}$appy liked to collect things. He had brought home small stones he found and polished them until they sparkled. He collected feathers, pine needles, wood shavings, and wildflowers from the woods. He saved scraps of cloth for sewing, and he had been saving string for a long, long time.

As Happy gazed at the sparkling stones, a picture of Snow White came to mind. He imagined her wearing a ball gown and a long necklace made of his stones, tied together with his saved string. "That's it!" he exclaimed.

Happy had just begun to work when
Sleepy asked him what he was doing.

"I'm making a gift for Snow White," Happy
explained.

"That's a good idea," said Sleepy, yawning.
"Will you help me make one, too?"

"Of course," said Happy.

$\mathcal{H}$appy and Sleepy piled pine needles onto a piece of cloth. They rolled the cloth up and tied the ends. Now the Princess would have a tiny, fresh-smelling pillow to put under her regular one at bedtime.

$\mathcal{N}$ext, Sneezy wanted to make a gift.
So Happy helped him carve a wooden whistle
that Snow White could use to call her bird friends.
Then Happy gave Sneezy a piece of string.
"Snow White can tie the whistle around her neck,
so she won't lose it in the woods," Happy said.

Happy gave Doc some bird feathers to tie together for a feather duster. Happy also gave Dopey strips of birch bark that Snow White could use to mark her place in storybooks.

Grumpy and Bashful soon asked Happy how they could make presents, too. So Happy helped them weave vines and string into a basket.

Before long, all the Dwarfs were making presents, then decorating them with pieces of Happy's string. All the Dwarfs were busy— all except Happy.

Because Happy had been so generous with his collections, almost everything was gone.

*O*nly one short piece of string was left.

Happy still had his box of sparkling stones.
So even though there wasn't enough string for a
necklace, maybe he could make a bracelet.

That evening, all the Dwarfs were tired. One by
one, they went to bed. Happy thought about the
beautiful bracelet he would make tomorrow.

*T*he next morning, Happy got ready to make the bracelet while the other Dwarfs finished their gifts. Then Doc told him that Bashful wanted string to wrap his present but was too shy to ask.

"Sashful is bad," Doc said. "I mean, Bashful is sad."

$\mathcal{H}$appy wanted to be generous to Bashful. "But if I give up the string, I won't be able to make my bracelet for Snow White," Happy thought.

"*I* want to help, Doc," Happy said. "But I've already given away everything except my sparkling stones and this little piece of string."

Doc nodded. "I know you've been gery venerous. I mean, very generous."

$\mathcal{M}$eanwhile, Snow White's royal carriage stopped just before the cottage. She thanked the coachman and headed for the Dwarfs' door. But as Snow White passed a window, she heard Happy and Doc talking. She understood the hard choice Happy had to make and wanted to help.

What would a princess do?

"*I*'ll tell Happy that he has already given me the best present of all," Snow White decided. "His gift is his generosity towards the other Dwarfs."

$\mathcal{B}$ut before she could knock on the door,
she heard Happy say, "Here, Doc, take the string.
I want Bashful to be happy."

Snow White waited a few minutes so
Bashful could wrap his gift. Then she knocked.
"Hello!" she called.

The Dwarfs rushed to greet her. Each one
proudly held up a gift—all except Happy.
Each gift had a tag.

Sneezy's gift tag read FROM SNEEZY AND HAPPY. Grumpy's tag said FROM GRUMPY, BASHFUL, AND HAPPY. The other tags also had Happy's name.

"Happy helped us all," Sleepy explained. "Then he couldn't make his own present. So our gifts are from him, too."

As the other Dwarfs put away the gifts from Snow White, Happy promised her, "I'll make you a necklace when I have more string."

Snow White smiled and hugged him. She reached into her basket and pulled out a large ball of string. A tag tied to it read FOR HAPPY.

"I've been saving this just for you," she said.

The End

For Happy
♥
Snow White

From BOBFUL and HAPPY

From SNEEZY and HAPPY

From DOC and HAPPY

From SLEEPY and HAPPY

From GRUMPY, BASHFUL, and HAPPY